A NOTE TO PARENTS

When your children are ready to "step into reading," giving them the right books—and lots of them—is as crucial as giving them the right food to eat. **Step into Reading Books** present exciting stories and information reinforced with lively, colorful illustrations that make learning to read fun, satisfying, and worthwhile. They are priced so that acquiring an entire library of them is affordable. And they are beginning readers with an important difference—they're written on four levels.

Step 1 Books, with their very large type and extremely simple vocabulary, have been created for the very youngest readers. **Step 2 Books** are both longer and slightly more difficult. **Step 3 Books,** written to mid-second-grade reading levels, are for the child who has acquired even greater reading skills. **Step 4 Books** offer exciting nonfiction for the increasingly proficient reader.

For my mom and dad
–K. C.

For Samantha
–A. C.

 Published in the United States by Random House, Inc., New York, and simultaneously in Canada by Random House of Canada Limited, Toronto.

Library of Congress Cataloging-in-Publication Data
Cristaldi, Kathryn.
Baseball ballerina / by Kathryn Cristaldi ; illustrated by Abby Carter.
p. cm. – (Step into reading. A Step 2 book)
Summary: A baseball-loving girl worries that the ballet class her mother forces her to take will ruin her reputation with the other members of her baseball team.
ISBN 0-679-81734-4 (pbk.) – ISBN 0-679-91734-9 (lib. bdg.)
[1. Ballet dancing–Fiction. 2. Sex role–Fiction. 3. Baseball–Fiction.] I. Carter, Abby, ill.
II. Title. III. Series: Step into reading. Step 2 book.
PZ7.C86964Bas 1992 [E]–dc20 90-20234

Manufactured in the United States of America 10 9 8 7 6 5 4 3 2

Step into Reading

Baseball Ballerina

By Kathryn Cristaldi
Illustrated by Abby Carter

A Step 2 Book

Random House New York

SHARK
SHARK

Chapter 1: BALLET LESSONS

I love to play ball.
I play shortstop on a team
called the Sharks.
We wear neat hats
and cool green T-shirts.

Mom thinks baseball
is for boys.
She wants me to do
more girl things.

That is how I got stuck

taking ballet lessons.

I have pink tights

and pink slippers.

Mom puts a pink ribbon

in my hair.

She says, "Pink is for girls."

I hate pink.

BASEBA
SHARKS

In class I sit next to
my best friend, Mary Ann.
She is the catcher
for the Sharks.
Her mother made her
take ballet too.

Mary Ann and I have a deal.

We must keep ballet a secret.

If the other Sharks found out,

they would laugh.

They would think

we were wimps.

Madame is our teacher.
She is very old
and very strict.

Mary Ann said she saw
her smile once.
I must have blinked,
because I missed it.

Every class starts the same.

First we line up at the barre.

Then we practice the five positions.

First position.

Second position.

Third position.

I make a face.

There is only one position for me.

Shortstop.

Sometimes I pretend

I am up at bat.

Madame is our coach.

"Heels on the floor!

Shoulders back!

Point the toes!"

she shouts.

Who knows?

Maybe pointy toes

will help my swing.

Madame loves flowers.

Last week we were buttercups.

This week we are dandelions.

"Pretend you are a dandelion swaying in the wind," she says.

She waves her arms.

"Look, I'm stuck in a tornado,"
Mary Ann whispers.
She spins around and around
really fast.
I giggle.

Madame walks over to Mary Ann.

My friend is in trouble now!

But our teacher smiles.

"Very lively, my dear!"

she says.

Chapter 2:
RECITAL BLUES

One day after class
Madame has some news.
"In two weeks
there will be a recital.
You will get to dance
on a big stage."

I feel like I just

got hit with a line drive.

I do not want to dance

on a big stage.

I do not want to dance

on any stage.

What if someone sees me?

What if the <u>Sharks</u> see me?

They will think I like

girl stuff.

They will not want

a ballerina for a shortstop.

Madame puts her arm

around Mary Ann.

She tells the class,

"You will be doing

The Dance of the Dandelions.

Mary Ann will be Queen Dandelion."

Everyone claps.

They pat my friend on the back.

"Too bad," I say to Mary Ann.
But she looks happy.
"I wonder if I get to
wear a crown?" she says.

For the next two weeks

we get ready for the big night.

It is worse than I thought.

We have to wear green tights
with lace on them.
We have to wear big,
fluffy hats.

I flap my leaves at Mary Ann.

"Look at me," I say.

"I'm wilting!"

But she does not laugh.

Something strange is
happening to my friend.
It started when Madame
chose her to be Queen Dandelion.
She does get to wear a special crown.
Sometimes she even
wears it home!

Chapter 3:

THE BIG NIGHT

It is the big night.
I am nervous.
I peek out from
behind the curtain.

I see my mother
and my baby sister.
Strike one!

I see my uncle Ethan
and my aunt Agnes.
Strike two!!

And then I see them.

They are sitting

in the third row.

They are wearing neat hats

and cool green T-shirts.

It is the Sharks!

Strike three!!!

"The Sharks are out there,"
I tell Mary Ann.
"They will laugh at us.
They will think
we are wimps."
But my friend just smiles.
"I hope they will like my crown,"
she says.

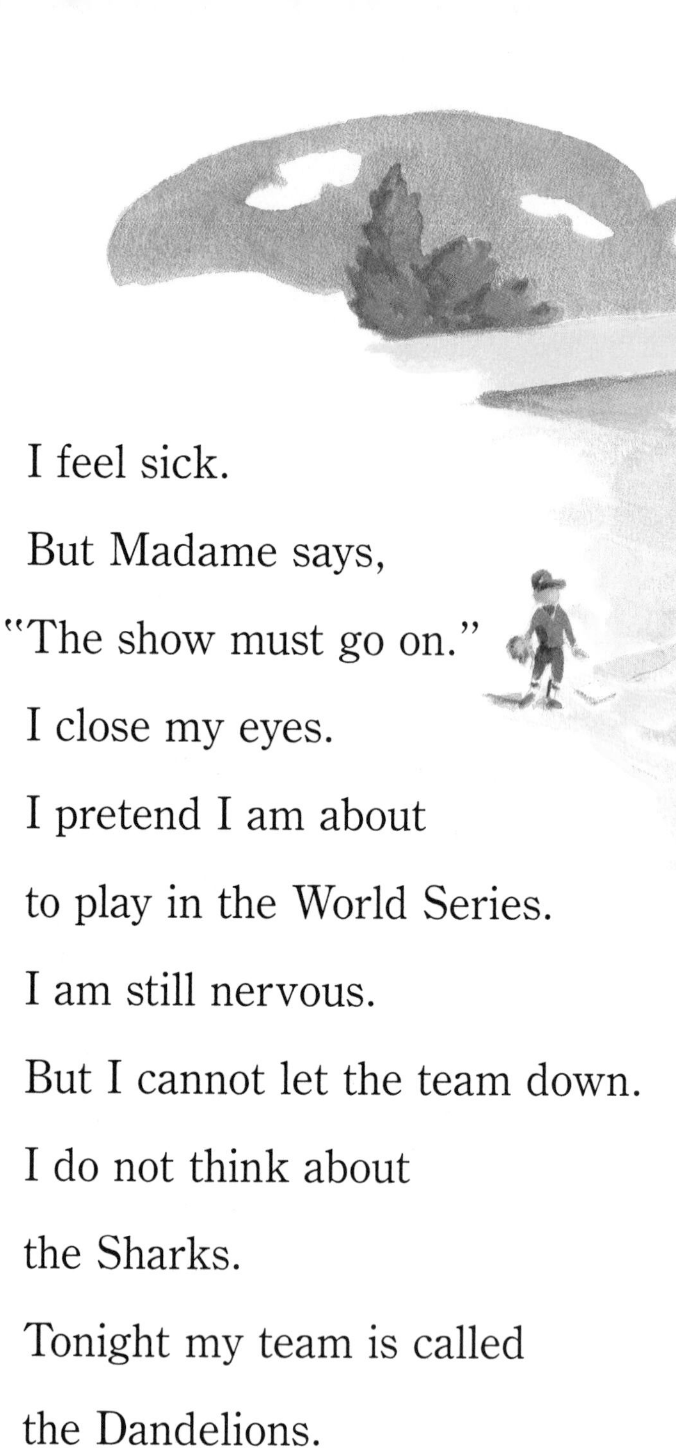

I feel sick.

But Madame says,

"The show must go on."

I close my eyes.

I pretend I am about

to play in the World Series.

I am still nervous.

But I cannot let the team down.

I do not think about

the Sharks.

Tonight my team is called

the Dandelions.

The curtain goes up.

Heels on the floor!

Shoulders back!

Point the toes!

Now it is time for

Queen Dandelion.

Mary Ann leaps on stage.

Suddenly her crown flies
off her head.
Up, up, up it goes!
It is a high pop.
The crowd gasps.
I dance across the stage.

I make the catch.

Everyone cheers.

Mary Ann giggles.

Afterward, the Sharks
give me high fives.
"You were great!" they say.
I feel like I just hit a home run.
Maybe ballet isn't
so bad after all.
But I still like baseball best!